HOUSE OF
TREASURES

BOOK 1

JOHN CHOPPER FRANKLIN

HOUSE OF TREASURES

iUniverse books may be ordered through booksellers or by contacting:

iUniverse
1663 Liberty Drive
Bloomington, IN 47403
www.iuniverse.com
844-349-9409

Because of the dynamic nature of the Internet, any web addresses or links contained in this book may have changed since publication and may no longer be valid. The views expressed in this work are solely those of the author and do not necessarily reflect the views of the publisher, and the publisher hereby disclaims any responsibility for them.

Any people depicted in stock imagery provided by Getty Images are models, and such images are being used for illustrative purposes only. Certain stock imagery © Getty Images.

ISBN: 978-1-6632-5066-7 (sc)
ISBN: 978-1-6632-5065-0 (e)

Library of Congress Control Number: 2023902960

Print information available on the last page.

iUniverse rev. date: 02/24/2023

BOOK I
THE TREASURE UNDER THE BARN

It all started with a boy from Ireland. He took two of his friends to an opening he found in a cave. They entered a new world they never thought existed.

They met kings, queens and creatures of all different shapes and sizes, With one goal: Peace for the world they live in. The wars they endured caused sadness for everyone.

The rescues they made and the lives that were saved were grand. The celebrations of victory they had brought them together to fight the evil side by side.

I wrote these books thinking of my own adventures in life with the memories from my friends. I hope you have a memory of your own to share.

John Chopper Franklin

This book is edited by Jenelle N. Franklin and dedicated to Pam Painter Franklin.

Contents

CHAPTER

1

THE DOOR TO THE NEW WORLD

It all started when I was a bright Irish lad. It was 1917. Times were tough, the potato farm we had was no more. Papa said the soil went bad. I was the youngest of five sons, Two died of the fever, one died in the war, and one married young. I never had any schooling, but Mama taught me how to read. Papa became a whiskey maker because it was the only way to make a shilling.

I got a job and made 10 cents a day working for a foreclosure company. When you didn't have the money to pay your debt, the company would move you out and sell or auction off all your property. I always felt bad when I saw the people being evicted, knowing that they had no place to go. The day I felt the worst was when we had to foreclose the property and kick out this one family. The daughter of the property owner was my sweetheart, Jezebell. She never looked at me wrong, but she always smiled at me. She had long red hair and pretty green eyes. When we looked at each other for what I thought was the last time, she was crying. I stood still for a second and was pushed over by my boss.

He hollered out, "You don't get paid for feeling sad, boy. Hit the stables and be quick about it!"

Every property we went to, I either cleaned the stables or cleaned the toilet house. I started at the horse stables and worked my way back to the chicken coops with my wheelbarrow and shovel. That was when I tripped and fell on some stones. When I stuck my shovel in the mud to pick myself up, the mud gave way and it hit something hard that made a hollow sound. I moved the dirt and mud with my shovel and found myself standing on what appeared to be a cellar door.

CHAPTER

2

THE ADVENTURE

I was very interested. I took my shovel and cleaned it off. I stepped back and figured out what it was. It was a wine cellar door! I opened it up and started to walk down the stairs. Every step I took, the boards on the sides of the stairs started to crack. All of a sudden, they gave way. I fell with a thud! I was knocked out. I woke up minutes later to my boss calling my name. "Tommy! Are you done with those stables yet?"

I hollered back, "I'll be done in a minute, sir!"

My boss hollered out, "You best be, or you won't get any supper." I made it out of the cellar and aimed 0n returning later that week. I closed the door and covered it with dirt. I cleaned the barn and took the bundle of lumber from the upper level down and outside for the rest of the crew to load it up on the trailer. My boss had a yard to keep the valuables taken from the houses he foreclosed. He sold them to construction companies. He made a penny on a nickel no matter how you looked at it! He was as smart as he was stubborn and believe you me, he was pretty stubborn in everything I could think of.

I got home and saw Mama on the porch crying. I ran up the yard and said, "Mama, what's wrong?"

She looked up at me with a sorrowful smile. "Tommy, your father has left the house and went looking for work up North. It will just be me and you for a while sweetie." Mama looked at me and said, "We're going to have some company for a week or two." I went in the house and got a piece of bread and glass of milk.

I heard a wagon coming up to the house. I looked out the window and was happy as can be. That's because the people in the wagon was Jezzy my sweetheart her mama and little brother Kenny. Jezebel's nickname was Jezzy. When Jezzy went to get out of the wagon she slipped. I quickly ran over and caught her in the air, and I fell in the smelliest mud puddle ever. Jezzy's mom saw what I did and smiled because her daughter was dry, and I was completely soaked in mud.

Jezzy stood up, held her nose with her fingers, and said, "Mama, now isn't he a gentleman?"

Her mama said, "A real stinky one, but a gentleman all the same."

Jezzy's papa went north with my papa to find work together. I went around the barn and jumped in the creek with my clothes on. I washed off all the mud and came to the house, where Mama gave me a shirt and a pair of shorts to get into. I went to the barn took off my clothes, I heard giggling. It was Jezzy, looking at my rear all bare. I stayed in the barn for about fifteen minutes because my face was all red from embarrassment. They shacked Jezzy's little brother Kenny up with me, and the girl of my dreams slept with her mama. I was paid for the week of work. I had done and gave Mama 65cents. The 65 cents bought a bag of brown sugar and yeast for the bread. Morning came and Mama made oatmeal for breakfast. We had twenty chickens, four goats, and five ducks, make those four ducks after dinner that night. Mama got five cents for a dozen of eggs, and she sold a couple dozen at the market every morning.

The next morning came, I was on my way out the door. Jezzy caught me at the door, gave me a kiss on the cheek, and said, "Thank you for letting us stay at your house for the next week. Is there anything I can do to thank you?"

I looked at her with a smile and said, "You just did."

She turned pink in the face and ran into the house.

Mama said, "Tommy, you best hurry home after work." Mama saw Jezzy give me a kiss, and she couldn't get that smile off her face either. I went to Jezzy's house to finish up the renovation.

I walked by the barn, and I heard an eerie whisper. A voice said, "The treasure's inside, Just open your eyes."

Talk about feeling excited, rich, and scared all at once. At work, I was the youngest of the five guys who worked for Tom the boss. Todd was Tom's son. Mike was a big and strong guy. It looked like he could easily put a horse on his back and tap dance like the horse was a feather. Mike was my best friend. No matter what the question was, Mike always had an answer, and most of the time he was right. Whatever he said, made me feel good about myself. And there was Micky. Micky couldn't talk because of a fever he had when he was a kid. One thing was for sure, Micky was the smartest person I ever knew.

That day, we finished up early and Tom gave us all a bonus I got 80 cents! Tom said he would be gone for two weeks. Tom was going up north to pick up some farm tools. He left with his son.

I looked up at Mike and said, "I gotta secret to tell ya. Wait until the guys leave." The guys all left.

Mike sat down on the porch and said, "What's up, big guy?"

I liked the way Mike said that because I was only 5 feet tall, and he was over six feet tall.

I said, "Well, you know the house we just did?"

Mike said, "That would be this one here?"

I said, "Yeah, and I'm sweet on the girl that lived here. And I think she is sweet on me."

Mike asked, "How's that?"

I said, "Because she gave me a big kiss this morning. Her family is staying over at my house until her papa finds work. It's pretty rough for work especially since all the potato farms went bad."

Mike said, "So your sweetheart lived here, eh?"

"Yes, she did," I said.

Mike said, "Let's have a look at her room." We walked in her room and automatically Mike said, "Now if you're looking for another kiss hop up on my shoulders." I was a bit confused, But I hopped up on his shoulders anyway. He spun me around and came to the window. "All right Tommy, take down those window curtains." It was a matching pair of homemade curtains with lace and silk sewed on it. I took them down and hopped off his shoulders.

Mike was like my brother. He reminded me of my brother Mark who died in the war. I could tell him anything and Mike could turn anything wrong and make it right. We walked our ways toward home, but before we parted ways Mike wanted to know if I wanted to go fishing in the morning. I said, "Sure! I'll meet you down at Whompers Creek."

I got home, opened up the door, and Mama, Jezzy, and her mama jumped out and said, "Happy Birthday!" I completely forgot about my birthday! It was great. I was thirteen and most important, I was the man of the house. We sat down and had stew for dinner. Then came the presents! I got three pairs of socks, and two leather shoelaces.

We had cake, and after we were done with dessert, I said, "I have a present for you, Jezzy. Come outside and I will show you." I went to the corner of the porch, picked up the curtains, and put them on my shoulders. Jezzy came out, looked at me, put her hands on her mouth, and started to cry.

I quickly said, "Are you okay?"

She said, "Yes, yes, I'm okay."

I asked, "What's wrong?"

Jezzy said "It's just, my grandma made these for me on my birthday."

I'm sorry for making you sad, and Jezzy said, "No you didn't Tommy, you made me happy! I thought I would never see them again."

She ran over to me, and sure enough, Mike was right, she gave me a big ole kiss, a hug, and a smile. She quickly turned around and ran back into the house, hugged her mama, and told her what I did for her.

Mama heard, she came outside and said, "Boy, you done made that girl the happiest thing on this Earth."

"I know Mama, I'm going to put a smile on your face too."

I gave that 80 cents that I got for the week to her. She said, "How did you get this for 2 days work?" I told her about the bonus and the time off. Before we headed inside, I mentioned I would be up early, because I was going fishing at Whompers Creek with Mike.

The morning came and once again, I met Jezzy at the barn I was holding two fishing poles. She said, "I heard you're going fishing."

I said, "That I am, and something else too."

She said, "Oh, what's that?"

"Well, it's a secret. I found something in your barn." I went up to the second level of my barn and dropped a burlap bag down. Jezzy was interested in what it was, so she asked me. I replied, "It is a long, thick rope."

She gave me a puzzled look and said, "What is it for?"

I said, "You're going to find out." We headed down to Whompers Creek. I didn't know why it was called Whompers Creek, but I was soon going to find out.

Mike had a pole in the water when we arrived. He saw me and Jezzy coming down the trail. As we got closer, we noticed he was smiling. He hollered, "Who's your friend, Tommy?"

Jezzy stepped out and said, "Kimberley Jezebell, but everyone calls me Jezzy."

"Well, what's in the bag Tommy?" Mike asked.

I quickly said, "A rope."

He said, "Why do you have a rope?" I told him to pull in his pole and follow me. We walked up to the barn and before we walked in, I paused and turned to Mike.

"I asked you to come because I trust you like a brother". We walked in. I held up my hand and said, "Stop here!" They both stopped. I carefully walked forward and moved the dirt that was covering the door on the ground.

Mike and I took the rope and tied it to a pole that was connected to the barn. It was called a lever pole and went all the way from one side of the barn to the other. As it turns out, the lever pole kept the barn from collapsing. I waved Mike over. We both looked down the hole and saw the collapsed staircase. Mike asked what happened and I explained that it broke while I was walking down the steps.

I lit up a lantern, tied the rope around my belly, and said, "I'll go first, then you Jezzy, and then you Mike." I got down in the hole and just kept going down and down. After what seemed like forever, I saw an opening that looked like a cave. I swung myself from one side to the other and jumped in. I hollered up, "Okay Jezzy, come on down. Just keep coming down until you see me." I threw the rope out to be pulled up.

Down came Jezzy. When she swung herself into the cave, she fell on top of me. It was great.

We were nose to nose, both of us smiling. I said, "Could you get off me I can't breathe." It seemed like she could have stayed that way longer, but we were on our first adventure. She rolled off me giggling. I put the rope out and told Mike to come down. As he was coming down, the old lever pole started to crack. Just as I saw Mike's shoes swing into the cave, I heard a big bang. The lever pole had broken, and it was coming straight down fast. Mike was right in the middle. I grabbed Mike's shoes and pulled him inside. I quickly hollered at Jezzy to get back. I pulled him in, and the barn's lever pole came crashing down. I quickly untied the rope from Mike's belly and right as I did, the lever pole went crashing through and took the rope with it.

Mike looked at me and said, "Wow! Now I think I owe you one!" All 3 of us shook the dirt off and Mike said, "Well, look what we have here!" He lifted his hand up and had something in his fist, It was a torch. I took it from him, took a match from my pocket, and lit the torch.

Jezzy said, "It looks like we won't need this," and blew out the lantern. We all started walking into the cave. We went for a long walk and then came to a wall. There was writing on the wall. It was a riddle and it said, "If you have come from the top and can't return there, look under the rocks, you will find the key there. The key has a note, it's a C you see. Find what it means, and the door will set free."

CHAPTER

3

THE JOURNEY BEGINS

We all stepped back, and Mike tripped on a board. I gave my hand to him. The board moved and uncovered some peculiar stones. Both of us looked at the riddle, then at the stones on the ground, and we smiled at each other. We had figured it out.

The first part of the riddle was solved. We dug through the rocks and came up with a bar. It looked like a fork but only had two tines instead of four. It had letters on it.

Jezzy giggled at us because we looked so confused. She said, "You don't know what it is do you?" We both shook our heads. Jezzy explained, "Mama calls it a tone bar. They used it to tune the church organ. Let me see it. You see those letters? The letters are notes, like a note B and a C for a note."

Mike said, "Wait a minute." They looked at the riddle, It mentioned C note. He looked on the tuner and it had a C on it. The wall had a small hole on the side, the tone bar fit perfectly.

Then Jezzy said, "Okay, let me see it." She picked up this piece of metal that looked like a long nail, held it in the light and hit the C note hard with the nail. The tone bar made this screeching noise. She got halfway in the hole and all of a sudden, the key was sucked it in.

The wall started to shake. I quickly grabbed Jezzy and pulled her back as the wall fell over. She said, "It looks like I owe you one, Tommy."

I looked at her, gave her a wink and said, "We'll figure out something later." Right when we stepped toward the wall, it started to shake and rumble. We all took two steps and jumped to the other side. Right as we jumped away from the wall, it swung up and returned to where it was when we came to it.

It was pitch black now and we didn't move. Mike lit a match and said, "This is the last match." He picked up the torch off the ground and lit the torch. We walked for at least an hour and a half. We heard like the rushing of a river. We saw a bright light at the end of the cave. When we got to it, all three of our mouths dropped. It was the most beautiful and unreal sight ever. That river we heard was actually a waterfall, but the waterfall was upside down! At the bottom of the waterfall was a lake. We looked above our heads at the ceiling. The ceiling was a wall of water with sparkling bubbles, with gold and diamonds in each one. Then there was this bright light, and four sparkling stars went over the pond and left a streak of four colors. It was like a beautiful rainbow.

CHAPTER

4

HOW TO GET ACROSS

After gazing at the bubbles and the waterfall falling upside down, we looked across to the other side and saw a little man come out of the rainbow. He was running with two pots of gold and disappeared into a cave in front of him. Mike looked at me and said, "I never thought I'd see an honest to goodness Leprechaun." We walked up to the shore and saw another riddle on a stone.

It said, "You've made it this far, I am happy to see, and you've seen my stars bright as can be! You want to go forward and don't know how. Just take two steps and you'll be on a ride. The ride you'll take will be wild and free. Hold your breath and soon you'll see."

Mike and I stepped back and tilted our heads to the left then to the right like two confused dogs.

Mike said, "Okay, this one look's confusing!" I nodded my head in agreement.

Jezzy giggled again and said, "This one is simpler than the last one."

Mike said, "Okay Jezzy, what does it mean?"

Jezzy said, "Do what I do."

We stepped back, as Jezzy walked to the shore. She took one step into the pond, turned her neck around, and gave me a wink. Right when she took the second step, she disappeared into the water!

I yelled, "Jezzy!"

I started to run toward her, and Mike stopped me. All of the sudden, I heard Jezzy scream, "Yahoo!" The waterfall disappeared, and she landed on the beach on the other side.

I hollered, "Are you okay, Jezzy?"

She looked at me and Mike and said, "I'm fine as can be Tommy."

With that I was on my way. I raised my hands, kept my eyes looking forward, took two steps, and disappeared.

Then I shot up the waterfall and hollered, "Yahoo" before I gently landed on the beach next to Jezzy. I hollered for Mike to take his turn. Mike took two steps and disappeared. He too shot up the waterfall and landed right next to Jezzy. We looked down and saw little footprints going to the cave next to us. They must have belonged to the Leprechaun. We decided to follow the footprints. The cave started to get smaller and smaller after a few feet we were crawling on our hands and knees. As we got farther into the depths of the cave, we started to hear music and laughter. We started to crawl on pebbles and metal that made this loud noise to the Leprechauns. The music stopped and so did the laughter. Right when we all got out of the cave, it looked like a ghost town.

There were houses on the hills and this big, long dinner table at the bottom, there was no one in sight. We got down to the floor by the dinner tables and Jezzy yelled, "Hello, is there anyone here?" The dinner table was full of food. We heard some rumbling under the table and at the end of the table we saw an engraving on the head chair. The engraving said *"Eddy Whompers."* Automatically, I thought of Whompers Creek. Jezzy looked under the table and saw this little boy shaking because he was terrified.

Jezzy got on her knees and said, "It's okay I'm not going to hurt you baby."

The little boy said "I'm not a baby!"

Jezzy came up and I asked her, "What did he say?"

"The boy said he was not a baby!" Jezzy went down and said, "I'm sorry I called you a baby. I have two of my friends with me. Can you come out and talk to me?"

He came out and said, "Why did you come out here?"

Jezzy replied, "Well, my best friend Tommy, he's the smaller one, found this cave opening in my grandpa's barn."

"Your grandpa?" The boy asked, "Is your grandpa's name Willard Gumphrey?"

"Yes, and my name is Kimberley Jezebell."

The boy ran out, hollering, "Grandpa, Grandpa, she's here."

He ran into a small cave and a minute later an older Leprechaun slowly walked out and said, "So your name's Kimberley, eh? What do they call you on the top?"

Jezzy said "everyone calls me Jezzy."

"And your grandpa's name is Willard?" Jezzy nodded yes and the Leprechaun continued, "He was the last human to come down here. I called him Willy, and he called me Skins. That's because I

15

pulled him back from falling into the creek down below. He said "I scared the skin off his teeth. He said he would name something after me."

Jezebell said, "He did. He named the stream on our property Whompers Creek."

Then the Leprechaun Skins said, "Well what do you know Willy came true to his word." Last time I saw Willy, it was longer than ten years ago. No one had come through that passage until you three did today."

Then Jezzy said, "I'm thirteen and a half."

Skins sighed and said, "How is that old coot?"

Jezzy told Skins she had never gotten to meet her grandpa Willy." Jezzy said "Grandpa died 3 years after I was born."

"Me and your grandpa were like the best of brothers."

Jezzy said, "Grandma always told me that grandpa was bonkers. Every time he came in late, he said he was drinking or fishing with his little buddy Skins." Skins sat back and I saw tears come to his eyes.

He said, "Old Willy, he was one of a kind!"

Grandma said "Grandpa didn't work a lick, but he paid for the property, the barn, the potato fields, and gave medicine to four families that got the fever."

Skins replied, "I gave your grandpa 3 wishes. He had to use the wishes for good will only, and that he did. Just a second. I want you to meet my family." He pulled a bull horn out from under his chair and blew it. That horn shook the plates on the tables. 5 seconds after the sound of the horn, all of the lights in the houses turned on and before I knew it, the tables were full of Leprechauns.

Jezzy introduced us, "This is my sweetheart Tommy and his best friend Mike."

Skins pointed across the table and said, "This is my wife Molly, and my daughter Jacky. And the one I named after Willy's favorite and only granddaughter, Kimberley Jezebell.

Jezzy put her hands on her knees and said, "Hello, my friends call me Jezzy, and I hope you will to."

"Well, Jezzy, my friends call me Kimmy, but you can call me Jezzy too."

Jezzy agreed, and said, "I think we need to have our own handshake." Jezzy stuck her pinky finger out and so did little Jezzy. They shook hands with their fingers and giggled. None of us had breakfast or lunch, sure enough, Mike was licking his lips looking at all the food on the table.

Skins looked up at Mike and said, "Well Mike, by the size of you, it looks like your mama feeds you pretty good. There are two kinds of people here. the fast and the hungry. Which one are you, Mike?"

Mike stood up tall and said, "I'm quicker than a rabbit in a carrot patch." Skins laughed and said told us to dig right in.

Skins said, "I never saw a man over six feet tall fall down and cross his legs so fast in my life." I laughed and sat down with Jezzy. We ate dinner, talked, laughed, and felt welcomed.

Then I said, "I have two things to say about this meal."

Molly quickly stood up and blurted out, "Now what's wrong with the meal, mister?"

"Well, the first thing is, please don't tell my mom this, but this is the best meal I ever ate. And the second thing is I ate so much I'm not going to be able to stand for at least an hour."

Molly looked at Jezzy and said, "Your sweetheart is a sweetheart!" Something kicked me under the table It was Skins. He gave me the thumbs up and a wink.

After we ate, Skins gave Mike and me each a cigar and a knife. I looked puzzled, Skins said, "Never smoked a stogie before, have ya boys?"

"No sir," we replied. He took the knife and cut off the end of his cigar. Mike cut his end off and I did the same.

"Now put those knives in your pockets," Skins said. He took a lit candle and sparked his cigar up we did the same.

The first puff Mike sucked in made him gag and cough all over the place. Skins looked at him and said, "You're supposed to taste it, not waste it."

I took a puff, blew it in the air, and said "It tastes pretty good."

Jezzy went up to Molly and Skins' house. Jezzy had to squat down to get through the door. She was then able to stand in the living room.

Molly said, "We haven't had a woman come through the passage in 70 years or more, and you are such a sweet well-mannered girl. I am 189 years old." Jezzy put her hand over her mouth in amazement.

Molly said, "Leprechauns have been known to live over 600 years. My husband Eddy is 265. I am his second wife. His first wife died. She fell 600 feet off a cliff. Eddy didn't marry me until 50 years later. Now I see the way you look at Tommy. Is he your chosen one for marriage?" Jezzy turned pink in the face. She saw two pictures on the wall of boys and asked who they are.

Molly said, "Those are Eddy's and my boys. We think they both died in the war. But we never found Damon's body. Skins had this feeling Damon didn't die. It's been about 25years and he hasn't stopped looking for him thinking about him."

Jezzy said, "I am so sorry."

"We were sad for years. It was a long time ago."

Then Jezzy said, "Tommy lost 2 brothers to the fever and 1 in the war."

Molly looked out the window and saw Mike and Tommy having a good time smoking cigars with Skins. Molly said, "He's taking kindly to Tommy. Eddy is pretty stern."

Jezzy asked what stern meant.

Molly said, "few things he can be are stiff, with a very wild attitude and very, very stubborn."

Outside the house, Skins said, "I think you fellas should go back home."

I asked why.

Skins said, "There is another war coming."

Mike said, "I have no parents, no property, and no woman. The only true friends are sitting at this table. I would rather fight alongside my friends than anything else in the world."

I said, "I will stand by your side for what you're fighting for."

Skins said, "I gladly welcome you to the realm of the fighting Leprechauns." He pulled out a jug, poured 3 shot glasses full of liquid, and passed a glass to each one of us.

He raised his glass in the air and said, "From our brothers

to our mothers to our fathers to our lovers, we will shed blood together to fight the evil."

He took his shot glass and drank the shot in just one gulp. We did the same but coughed and gagged.

Skins laughed and said, "Willy called this stuff the best Shine he ever drank."

I asked Skins what exactly this war was about.

Skins said, "It all started 300 years ago, and what started it was greed. We have good and true neighbors to the North. Those people are called the Canapes and they live in the forest. They are mostly nocturnal. They sleep in the day and work in the night."

I said, "Oh, how did you meet them?"

Skins began, "Well it was just after a hard rain. My brother went out for some solid gold, He tripped over a Canape named Geyser sleeping in the middle of a swamp puddle." A Canape is able to jump 100 feet at a time. They looked like gigantic bumble bees, but Geyser had broken both his legs. My brother Frankie was a kind and very resourceful man. He rummaged through the meadow and got four large sticks. He broke two of the sticks in half and straitened Geyser's legs. He took off his jacket and stretched it then tied it between the longer two sticks.

"Geyser said to him, "Frankie I am twice the size of you and two times heavier. How are you going to move me?"

"Frankie said, "Tell me where your forest is."

Geyser told him it was two mountains and four meadows to the north. Frankie then licked his fingers and raised them into the air and said, "I should have you home in a rainfall." Geyser looked puzzled. Every time it rains when the sun comes out, a haze of colors appears. They call them rainbows and they're magical,".

From one end to the other, the rain started, and the sun came out. Frankie quickly tied Geyser to his body and all of a sudden, whoosh! At the start of the rainbow, Frankie took one step into the rainbow and the magical power sucked Frankie up with Geyser. They rode the top of the rainbow over the mountains, over two meadows, and Geyser gently landed on a meadow bog. Frankie came down like a heavy rock headfirst into the next bog. Geyser started to laugh. Frankie pushed his head out of the bog, and as he was spitting out mud, he asked, "And what do you think is so funny?" After clearing the mud out of his mouth, Frankie started laughing too.

Skins then said "Leprechauns are very strong." Frankie got under Geyser and picked him up over his head. Then Geyser heard an alarming noise. It was the howling of the Wolves. Geyser made this loud gurgle noise and there was a flash of a small light. Frankie shot a diamond over the mountains to the Leprechaun village and his pocketknife turned into a large sword.

Geyser said, "My elders should be here in a matter of seconds."

Skins heard a bull horn and said, My Leprechauns should be here soon too." Five of Geyser's friends came, and right when they picked him up, two wolf-like beasts with swords appeared within inches of them all. The Canapes came through the air, swinging their swords, and pierced the wolves, dropping them dead in their tracks. The Leprechauns and Canapes stood side by side fighting. One Leprechaun and two Canapes perished in that war.

They washed the Canapes' bodies to get the dirt and blood

off and put them on top of two mountains of wood. They do not bury their dead. They cremate them. We were all saddened by their deaths.

Then one of the Leprechauns stood up between both their bodies. It was Frankie and he said, "I see a lot of sadness. You should not shed tears for the men that have perished. You should be happy because of the joy they have brought to you, because of the food and drink they have eaten with you, and because of the laughter! Please be not afraid to stand up and tell your friends a story about him."

There was silence for 10 seconds then a little boy stood up and said, "My father took me fishing. I caught three and Dad didn't catch any." His Dads' friends stood up laughing. Then the wife of a soldier who died stood and talked about the time she was proposed to.

Frankie stood up and said, "Let's have music and let us eat and drink and talk about the good and the bad we had with our comrades." They each shared fond memories of brothers and sisters from both clans, and it was peaceful for the next 500 years."

Skins said, "I got a visit from the king of the wolf creatures recently, and it wasn't good. That was two suns ago. I told him I would tell the others. We should be ready to battle in four suns from now. I've contacted many clans but only 3 can battle."

"Who are all the clans?" I asked.

Skins said "The first is the Stargazers. They are 1,000 strong. Next there's Mika he's the leader of the fighting unicorns and 1,000 of them are ready for battle right now. Lastly, the Dweller Mights, whose way of battle is their claws. Their claws are made of solid stone and the way they battle is underground. They dig holes and trenches over a thousand feet deep and leave four inches of the earth on top. When the enemy steps on the earth above, they fall to their deaths. We sent message to Kibby. There were over a 1,000 strong of her clan. The Dweller Mights' army is more than 3,000. As for the Leprechauns, there are more than 2,000 of us. Our weapons are swords, spears, daggers, and bows and arrows. All of them are made from diamonds and silver and more of them are gold."

I looked at Skins and said, "The woman in your house I want as my wife."

Skins said, "You boys follow me." We went to this cave. He said, "Step on in."

We opened the doors and covered our eyes because of the light. It was like looking into the sun. We slowly uncovered our eyes. From one side of the wall to the other was covered with gold, diamonds, silver, and jewels. Skins looked at Mike and said, fill two pockets and say no more."

Mike was silent and started to fill his front pockets. Skins told me to follow him deeper into the cave. "How old are you?" Skins asked." I said, I'm 13."

"So, you became a man and want to marry Jezebell?"

"Yes, I do"

Skins said, "I will give you 4 things." He handed me a crystal ball with a ring on top. "The moment I saw you, I knew you were one to become family. I am giving you the same as I gave to Jezzy's grandpa, three wishes. Every wish you make has to be honest and true, not for bad, just for good."

I looked at Skins and said, "My first wish is for our potato fields to become bountiful again, so our fathers may come home. My second wish is for my friend Micky. I wish he could talk because he lost his speech before he was one year old from a bad case of the fever." I didn't use my third wish. I walked up to Skins' house and called Jezzy. She came out. Right as I was going to ask her to marry me, there were horns blown from miles away and horns started to blow in the village.

Skins yelled "The war is on!" All of the children ran to their homes. I saw the women hugging and kissing their husbands. Skins looked at me and Mike and said, "Are you sure you are ready to fight?"

Mike said, "Yes Sir! Where's my weapon?" I was standing behind him, ready to follow. There were more than 1,000 Leprechauns at the end of the village.

Skins got up on a rock and said, "We're ready to leave and some won't come back. Are you ready to do battle, fight, and attack?" They all yelled with their swords in the air. Skins said, "Kelly's clan was more than 500 and they will stay behind to guard the Leprechauns' village."

They all went up and over the hills into the forest line and surrounded their gates. We marched for six hours.

Skins said, "What we need is rain."

There was a rumble and a shaking on the ground below. suddenly, a hole appeared, and a seven-foot fur ball jumped out and rolled to one side. His legs and arms popped out and then a head appeared he looked like a giant mole. It made a screech and said, "I am looking for Skins, Is there one amongst you?"

Skins came out and said, "Nickster? Is that you? Turn that butt around and show me that scar."

The giant creature said, "I am Nickster jr."

Skins said, "You see, about 50 years ago I met Nickster. We got drunk and tripped over a log and landed on the whiskey jug we were drinking from. Half the jug splintered and a big piece of it went right into Nickster's rear. I got a big piece of it out."

Nickster jr. said, "I got the rest. So why are you here with so many of your clan? Is the war on?"

Skins said, "Yes, it is."

Nickster Jr. said, "Just a minute. I will get Dad."

Skins told me, "The last thing you want to do is call Nickster king. Nickster's older brother was to be the next in line to become king. A war was on, and he died saving Nickster's life. He felt he never would take his brother's place as king of the Dweller Mights. They were also called the Cave Dwellers, but he hates to be called King Nickster."

It wasn't a second later before Skins said, "Get ready, because if I know Nickster, the ground will shake."

The first thing I heard was this mean voice that said, "I was feeling good because I thought you were dead." Then this huge ten foot tall fur ball came out at us and landed on Skins.

I heard Skins laughing and hollering, "When the heck are you going to take a bath. You still stink as bad as you did 50 years ago." They gave each other a big hug.

Nickster looked down at Skins and said, "I knew the war was coming. We are ready. How many do you have?"

Skins said, "Kelly's Clan is guarding the village and I have more than 600 with us."

Nickster asked how many days before battle and Skins told him five days. Nickster said, "We'll get drunk, be merry for tonight, and be ready before the sun rises tomorrow. I've have 800 ready for battle. Five of my scouts went to find out what we're up against."

Skins asked how many the other side has.

Nickster said, "Over 5,000 of the Wolf Clan, 700 hundred of the Karrik Clan, and 1,000 of the Drackle Clan. The Karrik Clan is still growing."

The Wolf Clan were half human and half wolf. They stood 15 feet tall on their hind legs. The Drackles were a new enemy; they had four lizard tails. They also brought a companion of war. They were called Kuzzlers. They were solid black unicorn horses with horns that turned into swords. All in all, there were 5,000 and the numbers were still growing. We had 2,800, not including Kibby and the Kibblers.

It was an amazing sight when we reached the bottom of the hole of Nickster's kingdom. There was a city of at least 10 thousand in his kingdom. It was just plain amazing to see! All of the Leprechauns came down the hole for the night and befriended the Dweller Mights. Skins and I were by the last fire of the night. Nickster and Skins were talking about how they were going to battle.

Nickster said, "I sent two scouts to find Kibby and her Clan, but they haven't returned yet. I'm sending another scout to find out why."

CHAPTER

5

THE FIRST BUT NOT THE LAST

Nickster gathered his Army and we all met at the top of his dwelling. We had two armies waiting together. The Stargazers were coming from the South and king Mika and his clan the Ukraine's were coming from the west. Nickster said king Mika will meet us at the battlefield.

A Scout came up to Nickster and said, "The Stargazers won't be here. Half of the army has died of the plague."

Nickster dropped his head in grief and shook it from the left to the right.

Nickster said, "I'll have food and medical supplies sent to them after the war is over. King Mika of the fighting unicorns will help without a problem."

We marched for two and a half days until we got to the meeting point of the armies. We saw that we had more help than we originally thought. There were 100 clans on our side and more clans were on the way. Mika, the leader of the Unicorns, was talking to the Kannaks. Skins and Nickster went to them, and they talked about their attack. The Kannak leader was called King Mokeetes.

King Mokeetes said, "We are strong and ready to fight." Half were on the ground with us, and half would ride in the sky on Mika and his Unicorns. The Ukraine's and the Kannaks lived side by side for more than a thousand years. King Mokeetes asked, "Have you heard from Kibby and her Kibblers?"

Nickster said, "No, we haven't." Then Nickster hollered, "Gabes, where are you, Gabes?"

There was a rumbling in the ground. A Dweller Might popped his head up and said, "Nickster, we are almost ready!" Then he pointed to the field where we were going to battle. Gabes made a loud bark and fifty more Dweller Mights came out of the ground. They started running to the center of the battlefield. 500 Dweller Mights were on one half and 500 were on the other. In a matter of a second, they all disappeared into the ground. Nickster, and his clan looked like 10 foot moles they were huge and ready for battle.

They dug three long trapping holes side by side. I looked in the sky and saw a Ukraine in the air. It landed quickly and ran up to Mika. Mika turned and told Nickster and Skins that the enemy would be there in ten minutes. In total, the evil clans were more than 10,000 strong.

CHAPTER

6

THE BATTLE
HAS BEGUN

I looked at the battlefield and saw a Drackle. Skins got on Mika, and they met the Drackle halfway down on the field.

The Drackle said, "Skins, what a pleasure to meet you! I've heard so many great things about you and your clan. I want to make peace and shed no blood." The Drackle's name was Spinstar. He then said, "So, spare your weapons and leave your land or perish by the sword in my hand."

Skins said, "If it's war you want, war is what you'll get."

Spinstar flew back and shouted to his creatures, "Blood is what you want!"

All of the evil Clans screamed, "Kill! Kill! Kill!" Out of the woods came 1,000 creatures followed by the others. They all were at a full run and fell into the trap holes that the Dweller Mights made. They did not stop, they created ladders with their dead and made a bridge to cover the traps. The Drackles and the Kuzzlers came ripping through with the Wolf Clan. Horns were blown on our side and that started the stampede. It wasn't even a few seconds before the fighting started and the Ukraine's took to the air, with Mika and his unicorns in front. King Mokeetes clan were on their saddles. The Kuzzlers attacked Mika and his unicorns in the air.

Fighting alongside the Kuzzlers were more evil clans, the Kerricks and the Stickers. The Dwellers were taking them out with the holes they made and crushing them with their stone claws. Mike was battling well when a Stickmite dropped from the sky and landed on his head. A split second later, an arrow shot right through the Stickmite. Mike looked and saw Skins with an empty bow. Skins winked at him, and then returned to fighting.

I looked up and saw a Kuzzler coming down at me. Just before he hit me with his horns, 5 golden arrows hit the Kuzzler in the side, and the Kuzzler dropped dead. I had been saved by the Leprechauns!

The war was getting worse as it went on. The Ukraine's were being shot down by the Stick mites, who were shooting through the air with bows and arrows. There were still hundreds of Unicorns, and they were fighting on the ground side by side like brothers to the end.

I looked to my right and saw Skins, it was bad. He was attacked by two Wolf creatures. Skins quickly pulled his knife from his side and jabbed it through one of their hearts. The other knocked him down. Right as the wolf took his tail to stab Skins in the heart, There was a scream in the air. It was Mike. He cut off the Wolf's tail. When Mike landed, he hit a sword that was stuck in the ground from a previous fight. The sword went through Mike's shoulder.

Skins got over to him and said, "I guess we're even buddy."

They quickly laughed then Mike went to the side, took his sword, and cut a Stickmite in midair. Mike took his dagger out, threw it in the air, and killed two Drackles that were right over King Mokeetes and his son. The Drackles dropped dead. King Mokeetes looked Mike in the eyes and nodded a thank you. After that, Mike passed out with the sword in his shoulder.

We battled long and hard. It was looking bad because the evil clans were taking over. Right as we thought we had lost the battle we heard a scream in the sky.

It was Kibby and the Kibblers. They were giant eagles, and Kibby was their leader. To the right of her was her daughter Logann and to the left was her son Austin. There were more than a thousand of the Kibbler eagles and they all divided into thirds. Logann took three hundred, Austin took three hundred, and Kibby took the rest. She looked at Logann and said, "You know what to do."

Logann's whole clan of three hundred disappeared in a heartbeat. Kibby's and Austin's clans went straight into battle. Austin's clan attacked the Kuzzlers in the sky. Kibby's clan went to the ground. The Kuzzlers were dropping like flies. When Kibby hit the ground, the Kibbler eagle power was there feathers. The feathers turned into gold flying spears, they launched off their wings, and stuck their enemies in the chest. After an hour more of fighting, We had the enemy backed into the woods. They were retreating.

Just before they were at the tree line, there was a loud screech. It was Logann. She and her clan of eagles were making a wall out of the fallen trees in the forest below. The enemy was trapped, and in a matter of seconds, Logann and her clan appeared above them. Logann got to the top of the wall of the trees they built. The eagles then spread a green dust over them, and every evil living and dead demon was turned to stone.

Kibby flew over, landed before Nickster, and said, "How long has it been, twenty years?"

Nickster said, "twenty five."

Kibby looked at Nickster and said, "You still haven't taken a bath, have you?" We all laughed.

Kibby said, "I need fifty of your clan to dig a hole deep enough to bury the evil creatures."

Nickster smiled and hollered, "Apollo, take fifty and follow Austin." Austin flew to the center of the field. Apollo and the Dweller Mights dug a hole more than a thousand feet wide and a thousand feet deep. Austin and his clan collected all of the evil creatures' bodies and dropped them in the center of the hole. Then Nickster and his Dweller Mights looked down at the dead.

Nickster looked at Austin and said, "My friend, we have done it!"

A tear came from Kibby's eye as she watched twenty of her Eagles carry fifteen wounded and five dead from her clan. Kibby then said, "They all had good lives and will be remembered for a thousand years to come."

Skins said, "We lost fifty and a hundred fifty are wounded."

Kibby said, "We will take them all to your village."

Nickster lost ten Dweller Mites and thirty were wounded. Mika lost the most. one hundred and twenty unicorns died.

Kibby slowly went up to Mika and said, "We will bury them like kings tonight." King Mika looked at Kibby and dropped his head in grief.

I went down the hill to the ridge and heard my name being called. I ran over and found Mike in a pool of blood. I screamed for Nickster and Skins. They came running down to me.

Nickster looked at Mike and yelled, "I need a Hincher!"

I was confused. Apollo came down the hill with his legs tucked in. He was like a big rolling brown ball. He stuck his legs and arms out, stopping three inches from Nickster's hand. Apollo handed Nickster a leather sack with a red cross on it. Nickster stuck his claw in it and came out with a little bottle. The label read Hench. Nickster broke open the bottle and a liquid came out. Nickster put it into his claws. He quickly ripped the sword out of Mike's shoulder then covered the hole with his claws.

Mike let out a gasp of air. I thought he had died but he just rolled over, looked at Skins, and said, "So, we're even now?"

Skins started to laugh, and said, "I guess we are, big guy!"

CHAPTER
7
FARWELL TO
A FRIEND

In the field below, Austin, Logann, and their clan of eagles went to the forest. They came out with dried brush and trees, stacked them into a pile one hundred and fifty feet high, and put all the Unicorn bodies on the top. Then, Mika came down to light the fire. We were all around him and Mika stepped back from the fire. It was a bittersweet moment.

Mika lifted his head up and said. "I saw great warrior's perish for a cause that would stand for more generations to come." Mika got on his two hind legs. He stood tall, and then spread his wings from his body. Wing to wing was thirty feet across. I looked at Mika, he shed tears of sorrow.

Nickster, Skins, Kibby, and king Mokeetes came up to him and sat beside him. We all stood on the ridge and bowed our heads.

Skins got on a stone, looked up at all of us and said, "I'm looking at you all and what I see is a family. A family of brothers and sisters who came from miles apart from sunset to sunset to a battle for peace which we won. You fought side by side and protected each other. Now you can look to your side and find your brothers and sisters."

There was nothing but bandaging each other's wounds. Then all the clans joined around bonfires and had a good time.

Morning came and the leaders stood in the center, promising to meet and gather twice a year. The first time they agreed to meet would be at the upcoming Apple Fest.

Mika's clan went to the east, Kibby and the Kibblers went to the west, and king Mokeetes clan went to the south. Nickster's clan and Skins clan went north.

On the second night of our travel home, Skins, Nickster, Mike, and I sat around a fire. The others talked of the old days when they were young, dumb, and well mannered. It turns out the days of good manners weren't that many.

One of the boys looked at Mike and said, "Do you think those at home are worried about us?"

Skins said, "don't worry. King Mokeetes sent a member of his clan to tell your mothers and wives where you are." They were all relieved to hear that their families had been told.

We got to Nickster's village, helped bury his comrades, and decided to stay the night. The families of the dead soldiers cried, rejoiced, and showed their pride like nothing we had ever seen. That is because their loved ones perished in the great fight for peace. Morning came and we were all ready to go home.

Skins looked up at Nickster and said, "I will be back in three moons with a full jug of whiskey to share only with you. But I'm not coming back till you take a bath!" They both laughed and hugged like true brothers.

CHAPTER

8

THE ARRIVAL IS HERE

It took us two days of marching to reach the village. It should have taken only one, but it took longer since Nickster gave us so much whiskey to enjoy the night before. On the last day of marching, we looked like we were all wounded from the head up because we had piercing headaches from Nickster's apple whiskey.

We arrived at the village, and all I saw was women and children running to their husbands and fathers. I admired the sight.

Then I looked up and was tackled by Jezzy. She was panting and said, "I thought you died." She was so excited. I put her on the ground, put my fingers across her lips, and hugged her. Then she planted a big kiss on me that lasted for five minutes.

I looked up and saw Skins talking to the wives and children of the Leprechauns who didn't return. He looked down at the children, then up at the wives, and said, "They fought strong, and saved my life more than twice. Be proud of your husbands and fathers because they will be remembered as the warriors who kept the peace."

That day, we buried our brothers and celebrated victory with a feast. The meal was set at the long table, which was surrounded by families and friends. The feast was amazing.

Skins stood up on the table and said, "We traveled for days and became friends all the same." Skins stood up on the table. He raised his mug in the air, he said "To our brothers who perished in the fight for peace and will be remembered for centuries to come. Eat and be merry my friends."

Everyone cheered.

Skins raised his hand with a glass of wine and said, "Rejoice, be merry, and remember this night for a thousand years to come."

Right after Skins sat down, Jezzy stood up. She looked at all of us with a loving smile and sung a song that her grandmother taught her. It was a song that touched everyone's heart. I was never so proud of her. Just like the first night, we couldn't stop eating because the food was so good.

CHAPTER
9
KIBBY'S RESQUE

The following day I heard some horns blowing. I got up, looked outside, and saw Skins talking to Kibby, Austin and Logann. I went out to see what was going on.

Skins said, "Find Mike and Kelly and be quick about it!"

We got down there and heard Kibby needed two small and two tall men. Mike hopped on Logann's back and Kelly, and I hopped on Austin's. Skins joined alongside side of us, and we were on our way.

We were going so fast we couldn't talk. I looked down and saw Kibby's village. It took less than five minutes to fly from Skins' village to Kibby's. It would have taken us two and a half days to walk there. We met Kibby at the gate. She had a limp and looked very tired.

She said, "How ya doing Skins?"

"Skins said by the looks of it, better than you. Tell me what's wrong, friend".

"Three of our hatchlings are trapped in the tunnels below. And we are too big to rescue them."

Skins said, "Say no more, Kibby. How deep have they gone down?"

Kibby said, "More than a hundred feet."

Skins quickly said, "I need four ropes, each one hundred feet long."

The ropes were found and gathered in a matter of minutes. The ropes were tied to a boulder above us, and we were lowered down one by one. We got to about eighty feet and we heard hissing and rocks moving.

Skins looked up at us and said, "Be quiet." He looked at Mike and said, "We need weapons, swords, and slingers."

Mike tugged on his rope and was pulled up. Right when he reached the top, he told Kibby what Skins needed. He was given a satchel full of the weapons. When Mike was lowered down, he handed the swords and slingers to each of us and stepped into the cave next to us. We all followed Skins to the end of the cave and then looked down.

We saw the three hatchlings, all in cages, next to a big cooking pot over a fire. They were the meal for the night.

Skins said, "Kelly, Mike, go around to the other side and get ready for anything." That's what they did. Then Skins turned to me and asked, "Are you ready?"

I said, "Yes sir."

We climbed down the wall and jumped on the cages. Right when we landed on the cages, the hatchlings started to yell.

Skins put his fingers on his lips and said "Shh! Be quiet. We're here to rescue you!"

We cut the cage doors open. Skins put two hatchlings on my back and the third on his back. I got to the wall and climbed up. When I looked down, I saw Skins stepping off the cage, then two rocks fell down from the wall. The enemies who were going to eat the hatchlings were called Grunnelsnakes. One of them saw us. Right as he was going to blow his horn, Kelly shot a slinger that landed right between the Grunnels mouth and eyes.

Mike said, "Good shot!"

Mike and Kelly came around to meet us. suddenly, the Grunnelsnakes started dropping from all directions. We whipped out our swords and started to fight. There were hundreds of them. We were stabbing them with our swords from left to right. As soon we killed them, they turned to ash. It was weird, but when they died that is what happened to them.

It took us more than an hour to get to the end of the cave. Skins put the hatchlings into the satchel and sent them up the rope. That left three ropes.

Skins said, "You guys get up there now."

I was tied to one of the ropes. I had four slingers and a sword. I helped the others up to the top and returned to help Skins. When I got down to the beginning of the cave, there were Grunnelsnakes everywhere. They were on Skins' back and legs, but he was still swinging his sword in front of him.

And I had to do something fast. I threw the slingers on the Grunnelsnakes that were on his back and head, and they quickly turned to ash. I then took the extra rope, lassoed Skins, and took him out of the cave. I tugged on the rope, and we were pulled up faster than ever. When we got to the top, Kibby's eagles cheered and rejoiced.

The mothers were hugging their hatchlings with their wings. And of course, Kibby hugged Skins, Kelly, Mike, and me and then said, "Once again, Skins, you saved the life of my clan. Is there anything I can do for you, Anything at all?"

Then Skins stood up like he had hair on his chest and said, "Well, the boys and I are pretty hungry. How about a sandwich and a pint or two to drink?"

Kibby laughed with a smile, and said, "What's mine is yours! But you already know that."

Kibby climbed up on a rock and said, "Let there be a feast for our neighbors who once again saved the day."

They prepared a for us. We stayed for the rest of the day and then we were flown back to the village. we hopped off Kibby, Austin and Logann, Mike tripped over his own two feet, and we laughed right with him. Mike didn't drink one pint, he drank four.

Skins said, "Kelly you're going to have a guest sleeping in your barn tonight. Because The last thing I need is for Molly to smell liquor!"

It took us ten minutes to walk Mike to the barn stall. We took him to the front of the sheep pen. He tripped, landed on a pile of hay, and was knocked out for the night.

Skins and I went down to the creek and walked the shoreline. It was a nice walk. I told Skins that I was having the best time of my life, it has been non-stop excitement and adventure.

Skins laughed and said, "That's what Willy said, every time he came."

We got to Skins house real late. We saw skins wife with Molly asleep in the rocking chair on the porch and Jezzy was on the chair beside her. I quietly bent over, picked up Jezzy and carried her to her bed. Skins picked up Molly and did the same.

We went back to the porch and talked all about skins and willy's adventures almost until dawn. Eventually, we both went to our bedrooms. I walked into mine and saw Jezzy snuggled under the covers. I didn't want to wake her, so I laid down beside her and stayed on top of the covers. I put my arm around her she grabbed my arm and snuggled it across her heart.

Skins got to his room and laid down next to Molly. When he put his hand around Molly, she grabbed his arm hard, turned around, and said, "Do you know what time it is, mister? I stayed up all night worrying about you, and you smell like liquor!"

Skins was shaken but said, "Well for one, you didn't stay up all night. You were on the porch sleeping. I picked you up gentle as a dove and laid you to rest. I only drank half a pint. I smell like liquor because I helped Mike to bed after he had four pints. Oh, and it is breakfast time because I sure am hungry." Then Skins laid back on the bed and threw a blanket over his face. Underneath the blanket he was smiling. It was the first time in fifty years he had finally won an argument.

Let me tell you about Molly. She was the sweetest, loving, most caring Leprechaun you would ever meet, but she could be more stubborn and mean.

Molly got up, walked to the front of the bed looked at Skins with a smile, and grabbed the covers. She ripped them off the bed, looked Skins right in the eyes, and said, "If you think you have the upper hand in this discussion, you sir, have another thing coming!"

Skins' glorious smile turned into a guilty grin. Molly turned her back to Skins, opened up the door with a big grin, and walked out of the room.

CHAPTER
10
WHAT AN EYE OPENER

I woke up and heard singing. I got out of bed, came to the door, and stepped out. Skins came out of his room at the same time, looked at me, and right as he was about to say good morning, we heard a stern voice yelling.

"You two sit your rears at the table right now!" Jezzy was smiling at me in the doorway. Molly turned around and went back into the kitchen. Jezzy followed her.

I looked at Skins. He looked at me and said, "Don't ask." I didn't.

Molly came out with a big platter and Jezzy was right behind her with a pitcher of orange juice. Molly put the platter down and Jezzy set down the pitcher of orange juice. They sat down at the table with us and then came that mean voice. Molly looked right at Skins and me and asked, "Now where do you think those napkins belong?"

Skins and I grabbed the napkins in front of us and put them

on our laps. Molly took the lid off the platter and there was a meal fit for two kings. Eggs, bacon, pancakes, and every fruit you could think of. I never had a breakfast with so much food. It was delicious. Right down to the crumbs of the pancakes.

Molly looked at me and said, "So where is that friend of yours, Mike?"

What was good about that moment was that my mouth was full of pancakes and Skins' mouth was empty. I politely pointed at Skins to answer. He told her about the pints he drank, and how Mike had stayed in the barn with the sheep.

Molly said, "I want you boys to clean out the wagons for the apple harvest this afternoon."

Skins blurted out, "We'll get on it right after breakfast, dear."

We went over to Kelly's, where all of Skins' wagons were kept. We saw Kelly coming out of his barn laughing. When we got closer. Skins asked what was making him laugh so hard. Kelly told us to go in and take a look. We walked into the barn and saw Mike sleeping around a sheep. he had the biggest smile on his face.

Skins said, "Watch this kiddo!" He got down and put the sheep's head right next to Mike's face. The sheep started to lick Mike". Skins threw some hay on Mike's head and Mike still had this smile on his face. He opened his eyes, looked at the sheep licking his face.

Skins, Kelly, and I started to laugh so hard we fell to our knees. Mike jumped up, looked at the sheep, and didn't know where he was. Then had a big laugh with the rest of us.

We gathered all the wagons and cleaned them for the apple

harvest. We heard horns blowing from miles away and then Skins returned the same sound out of his horn.

I looked at Skins and said, "Are we going to war again?"

Skins and Kelly laughed. Skins said, "Oh no! Those are horns from Kibby, Mika, Nickster. and King Mokeetes. They are all going to meet at the center of the apple orchard."

Skin's clan had over a thousand wagons. All of the women were starting fires and gathering cooking pots.

I looked at Skins and said, "Is there going to be enough apples to fill all of those wagons?"

"We can fill those wagons a hundred-full," Skins said.

We saw smoke coming from over the mountains. Skins said, "I'm getting hungrier by the second."

I looked at Skins. I was puzzled until we got to the top of a hill and looked down. It was amazing. There were at least twenty square miles of apple trees. I looked toward the middle and saw a one square mile piece of land right in the center of the orchards. It had about ten fire houses in the middle.

Skins hollered, "Kelly, Mike, Tommy! On your horses." We got onto our horses and rode toward the middle of the orchard. We met Nickster and his son Nickster jr., and Kibby brought Logann and Austin. Mika brought all of the unicorns in his clan.

Skins said, "I see everyone is here except for king Mokeetes Clan."

Kibby looked at Skins and said, "The fever hit their village. King Mokeetes is strong. He met me on the outer banks and told me to tell you all that he will be here next year."

Skins looked at Kibby and, before he could say anything, Kibby said, "I have 2,000."

Mika said, "I have 3,000."

Nickster said, "With my clan of a thousand, together we will harvest enough food and medical supplies for two seasons to come for King Mokeetes."

Then Nickster blurted out, "Do the rules still stand?"

All of us laughed. About five hundred years ago, all of the clans' fathers made a pact that whoever found the largest apple and brought it to the middle fire house before sundown was the winner. All the Clans then had to give their first 100 jugs of apple whiskey to the winner.

Mika shouted, "Let's get it started"!

All the clans went into the center. Mika flew to the top of a hill and said, "I have two things to say. He bent his head and wings, and gathered some dirt from the ground, and said, "I'm looking at warriors, comrades, brothers, and our fathers from generations all walked on the soil I hold. Let this moment be remembered for generations to come, that our children can walk on the same soil we share."

All the Clans stood and cheered with one another.

Then Mika continued. "The second thing I have to say is, Nickster, our whiskey shelves are looking bare."

Nickster, Mika, Skins and Kibby laughed. Then the contest of fun began. It was an amazing sight. There where over 4,000 eagles, unicorns, Dweller Mights, and Leprechauns. They all disappeared from the center into the forest of apple trees. I never heard such laughter and fun between four different walks of life.

There were different ways of harvesting the apples. Nickster's clan was the fastest. Nickster and the older clan members were ten feet tall. They would put their legs, arms, and claws inside their fur. Three smaller Dwellers would roll them into the trees, and they would knock almost every apple off.

The unicorns did something different. Mika's clan of unicorns would stand eight feet away from tree, spread their wings, and with one whoosh of their wings, they would take down all of the apples.

Kibby would hover over a tree, grab the largest limb, and shake the apples down.

Skins and the Leprechauns just wheeled their wagons under the trees. They would all jump into the trees and drop the apples in the wagons below.

After five hours passed, all of us were pretty tired. We all gathered back to the center. Skins, Mika, Kibby, and Nickster were nowhere to be seen. We all heard grunting and groaning. We looked behind us and it was all four of them rolling their prize apples. These apples were huge. They rolled their apples up to the scales. Skins put his apple on first and it weighed twenty stones. Mika's apple weighed twenty five stones. Kibby's weighed twenty eight stones, and Nickster's weighed twenty eight stones. It was a tie. For the first time in 500 years, two apples weighed the same. It was decided that each would get fifty jugs instead of one hundred.

It was a great day. We all ate, drank, and sang. After the meal, the others took their crops home all except Kibby, Skins, Mike, and Nickster. I got on Mika, Skins got on Logann, and Mike, and I got on Austin. We flew the other way to help our friend King Mokeetes.

CHAPTER

11

TO LOOSE A FRIEND

We arrived at the foot of the hill. One of King Mokeetes warriors met us at the front and said, "If it wasn't for your medicines and food, we would have lost thousands."

Nickster asked the warrior, "How is your King?"

The warrior said, "He is in the castle, on the altar bed." That meant that King Mokeetes was dying. We walked through the village. It wasn't as bad as I had imagined. I thought there would be sick and dying people in the houses and streets. There were over five hundred freshly dug graves though.

We got to the castle doors, and they slowly opened. We looked at the bed and King Mokeetes loudly said to his servants, "Leave this room! Let me speak to my friends."

Kibby walked to his bedside first and bowed her head. King Mokeetes looked at her and said, "You have done my clan well with the food and medicines you've given to my people. To you I give the Diamond of Hope." King Mokeetes set the Diamond of Hope on Kibby's wings.

Nickster walked up next, and King Mokeetes said, "And to you Nickster, you taught me to smile, joke, and laugh with our brothers, both mine and yours. To you I give my Bracelet of Courage."

Mika came to him next. King Mokeetes said, "Your father lifted the stones on my castle. It was also your heart that gave us courage. To you I give the Sleeve of Peace." Mika bent his head down and King Mokeetes put the Sleeve of Peace on his horn.

Then Skins went to his bedside. King Mokeetes said, "And to my old friend Skins, do you remember when we first met?"

Skins said, "Yes I do, and that's because I won."

King Mokeetes coughed long and hard, then laughed.

When Skins and King Mokeetes first met, they were on the riverside and just boys. King Mokeetes was on one side of the river and Skins was on the other. They were both skipping stones across the water, and it turned into a game. Skins threw his last stone, and it skipped five times longer than King Mokeetes. King Mokeetes pulled out a stone, gave it to Skins, and said, "If I had this stone with me, then I would have won." They both laughed.

King Mokeetes looked at Skins and asked, "Tommy and Mike, are they still here?" Skins nodded yes, and King Mokeetes said, "Tommy step forward, said, The king "Tommy, you have been a great friend who stood by me in a time of need. I give to you the Ring of Fire, and I know you will use it well for a friend in need." I nodded in appreciation.

"Now, to the one who saved my life and my son's life in battle." Mike stepped forward. King Mokeetes said "My son has passed, and I will soon meet him in the heavens above. You are the man who saved my life and my people's freedom. I give to you my kingdom because I know you will serve it well." King Mokeetes took his sword from his side.

Mike fell to his knees and said, "I will serve you well my king." Just after King Mokeetes touched Mike's shoulders with the blade and laid his crown on Mike's head, the king died.

Skins stepped back and said, "All hail King Mike." We all bowed our heads to Mike. I never thought that my best friend would ever be a king. It was a grand day indeed. Mike was just a farm boy and was handed the crown to a kingdom of more than 10,000 people.

Mike stepped back, turned around, and looked at Kibby, Mika, and Nickster. Mike said, "I am going to need some help." Kibby and Mika flew into the air and Nickster went with them. They returned in half an hour with more than a thousand clansmen.

In a matter of three days, Nickster's army plowed Mike's fields. Mika's unicorns helped build back the towers that collapsed. Kibby's eagles gathered wood for housing and for heating during the coming winter. Kibby, Nickster, King Mika, Skins, and I met Mike at the gate.

I looked up on his kingdom wall and saw this huge ten foot by ten foot painting. The painting was a portrait of King Mike his wife, and his 3 children. Nickster said "Queen Pamela painted that picture."

Queen Pamela, her sister Queen Rixy and Queen Rixy's daughter princess Abriella were called the (Queens of design). Queen Rixy's power was fabric, she designed everything from the kingdom's curtains to the blankets they sleep on. Princess

Abriella's power of design was children's clothes. Queen Pamela's power was painting. All of the kingdoms in the underworld had her paintings on every Cathedral wall. She also had the power of design. She has been building and designing kingdoms for more than a hundred years with her sister Queen Rixy. I looked over and saw a thousand chariots in the sky flown by 10 foot tall butterflies, It was princess Rebecca and the rainbow riders.

The first chariot landed, and Queen Pamela stepped out. Then the next chariot landed, Queen Rixy and princess Abriella stepped out. There were over 1000 seamstresses with Queen Rixy and Princess Abriella. Princess Abriella started measuring the children for new clothes. Queen Pamela had more than a hundred children around her. For all that's happened to them. Queen Pamela put smiles on all their faces and asked the children if they could help her paint all of the houses. All the children had a great time When they were done it looked like a new kingdom.

Skins looked up at Mike and said, "You have a great responsibility now. I know you will serve them well. If you need anything, anything at all, I am to the North, Nickster to the south, Mika's to the west, and Kibby's to the east. We are all within a half day's travel to you."

Mike's eyes were watering. He looked at all of us and said, "Thank you, You all are, and forever will be, my friends to the end." Everyone left but me.

Mike and I looked at each other and I said, "You've got yourself a job now. Well, I guess this is goodbye."

Mike pushed me away with a smile and said, "This isn't goodbye, it's see you later big guy." We both smiled, turned around and walked our separate ways. I went up to where King Mika was, and we flew over the kingdom then went home. We landed and King Mika said he would visit King Mike to see if he needed help in the weeks to come.

CHAPTER

12

TIME TO SAY GOODBYE

We walked to the center of the village where all of the cooking was happening. We saw Molly and Jezzy looking right at us with smiles on their faces. Jezzy gave me a big hug and kiss and asked, "Where's Mike?" I took her aside and told her what happened.

Jezzy said, "It looks like we will be going home within a couple of days." Right as I was going to explain what happened to Mike, I heard this old Irish song being sung. Jezzy blurted out, "Oh my God!"

Skins turned and saw Micky, my friend who couldn't talk, and I remembered the second wish I made. It was for Micky to be able to speak and sing. He was walking with one of the Leprechauns, Skins' friend Kelly. He had gone up to the top, gave Jezzy's mama some gold coins, and returned with Micky.

Micky yelled, "Tommy, I can talk! I can sing!" I turned to Skins and Skins put his finger across his lips, it was a sign of secrecy. I could not tell anyone about my wishes. Micky ran up to me, gave me a hug, and said, "All of the fields are green and sprouting. Where's Mike?"

I told him about the war and the kingdom Mike had received.

Micky said, "Only Mike can get a prize like that."

I said, "Yes, a prize, but a great responsibility. I'm sure he would love to see you."

"The good news gets even better. Jezzy's papa and your papa will be home in two months. Both your mamas are okay and can't wait for you to get home. Your little friend gave Jezzy's mama ten gold coins. She paid off the farm and they are moving back into their house. Isn't that great!"

I looked at Skins and said, "Do you think we can give Micky a ride to see Mike?"

Skins said, "He looks a little hungry. Why don't you come in. We just put supper on the table." After talking for an hour Skins and I stood up and heard a noise. We left the table. Micky was talking and telling Jezzy and Molly a story.

Skins and I walked out and went to the top of the hill. I heard that noise again. It was a horn. Skins said, "That's Nickster's horn, Kelly call Kibby. Let's get over there." Then Skins looked at me and asked, "Are you ready for another adventure?"

I nodded.

Then Skins said, Let's say goodbye to the ladies."

Right when we got down to Skins' front porch, we met Molly with her hands on her hips. She asked, "Were those war horns, Skins?"

Skins said, "No, it's a call for help."

Then Molly said, "Tommy, you go in there and tell your wife-to-be what you are going to do."

Skins gave a whistle and Kelly appeared. Skins said, "Kelly, take Jezzy and Micky. They have to go home. Take them through the Whompers Creek passage."

Skins tossed Kelly a little sack. Kelly asked, "Is this memdust?"

Skins said, "Yes, it is, and it's only for Micky."

Kelly said, "only for Micky boss."

I went in the house and saw Jezzy with those beautiful green eyes looking right at me. She was crying and said, "You're leaving me again, aren't you?"

I answered, "Yes, I am. Kelly will take you and Micky home. You need to help your mama move your things back to the farm." I turned to Micky and said, "Micky, I need you to be by my girl's side, and do whatever she tells you to do, you hear me?"

Micky said "Yes, I do Tommy. And I will take care of the heavy work for both families."

Then I looked at Jezzy and said, "Jezzy, tell Mama I went south for two weeks to a moving job with Mike." I will send for you when I return."

She looked at me and hugged and kissed me. At the same time, we both said, "I love you."

We got to the front door and saw Molly holding two sacks. They were full of food and water. She handed them to Skins and me and said, "There will be no bloodshed, right young man?"

Skins smiled and said, "No there won't be, my love."

Then Molly said, "I trust and love Jezzy, but I don't know much about Micky."

Skins held her shoulders and said, "Don't fret, my dear. Kelly will walk them home and I gave Kelly some memdust for Micky." Molly gave a sigh of relief. Memdust is short for memory dust. Just a pinch of it will cause a person to forget. Anything the person remembered, would soon be forgotten the next day.

Skins and I went to the top of the hill. Two shadows came over the top of us and landed nearby. They were Kibby and Logann. Skins asked, "What's wrong, Kibby?"

She looked at Skins and said, "I don't know, but I know it isn't good. Nickster hasn't answered and Mika is meeting us at the Three Rivers Crossing." In a matter of seconds, I was on Logann's back. Skins was holding onto Kibby, and we flew over the sunset heading to Nickster's kingdom.

Thank you for reading Book I.
The House of Treasures.
John Chopper Franklin

Printed in the United States
by Baker & Taylor Publisher Services